An Imprint of Sterling Publishing
387 Park Avenue South
New York, NY 10016

First published in 2009 in Great Britain by Orchard Books, an imprint of Hachette Children's Books.

Text and illustrations © 2009 Sam Lloyd

This 2014 edition published by Sandy Creek.

ISBN 978-1-4351-5627-2

Manufactured in China

Lot #:

2 4 6 8 10 9 7 5 3 1

05/14

Inspector Croc
INVESTIGATES

Sam Lloyd

Sandy Creek
NEW YORK

The sun is shining in Whoops-a-Daisy World and at Catch-'em-Crooks Police Station, all is quiet. There is nothing to report – oh – except a pair of glasses have been handed in to Lost and Found.

Then, suddenly the calm is shattered! Ring ring!
There's an emergency phone call!

Inspector Croc takes the call. It's Rory Lion calling to say something is wrong in Whoops-a-Daisy World.

"Sizzling sirens!" gasps Inspector Croc. "Don't touch anything — I'll be there in a flash."
Inspector Croc is the cleverest animal in town. Whenever there is a puzzle, he can solve it.

Inspector Croc leaps into his police car.
Woo-woo-woo goes the siren as he races
through the streets. Everybody is very alarmed.
Whatever could have happened?

Inspector Croc screeches up at the crime scene.
"Someone knocked over my paint!" Rory Lion explains.
"What sort of scoundrel would make such a mess?"

"Please stay calm, sir," says Inspector Croc.
"Think carefully. Did you see anything peculiar?"
"I saw a curly tail," says Rory Lion.
"Hmm, very interesting," nods Inspector Croc, as he
examines the paint. There is a trail! It leads him to . . .

. . . Fix-it Fox. He's really cross!

"Someone has cycled into my concrete!" he cries.

"Only a real rascal would do such a thing."

"Please stay calm, sir," says Inspector Croc.

"Think carefully. Did you notice anything peculiar?"

"I did hear a loud 'oink!'" Fix-it Fox announces. "Hmm, very interesting," says Inspector Croc, as he examines the scene. He spots footprints that lead to . . .

. . . Moo Farm. Farmer Moo is fuming!

"Look at my crops!" he yells. "Only a real rogue would do such a thing."

"Please stay calm, sir," says Inspector Croc.

"Think carefully. Do you remember anything peculiar?"

"Yes, I saw a flash of pink," says Farmer Moo.

Inspector Croc needs to get back to the police station to crack the case before anything else happens. Never before had Whoops-a-Daisy World seen such mischief!

As night falls, Inspector Croc pieces together
the clues — curly tail, oink, pink . . .
Who would cause such a commotion and why?
Then something catches his eye . . .

The glasses! Of course! Suddenly the clues all drop into place. Inspector Croc realizes who is behind the peskiness! He must find that person, **quickly,** or who knows what might happen next!

Inspector Croc zooms through Whoops-a-Daisy World looking for the suspect. Where would the trail of destruction lead him? Uh-oh, it leads him to . . .

. . . Scary Wood!

A scream echoes from among the trees.
Quick as a flash, Inspector Croc leaps out
of his car and charges into the wood!
He isn't scared.

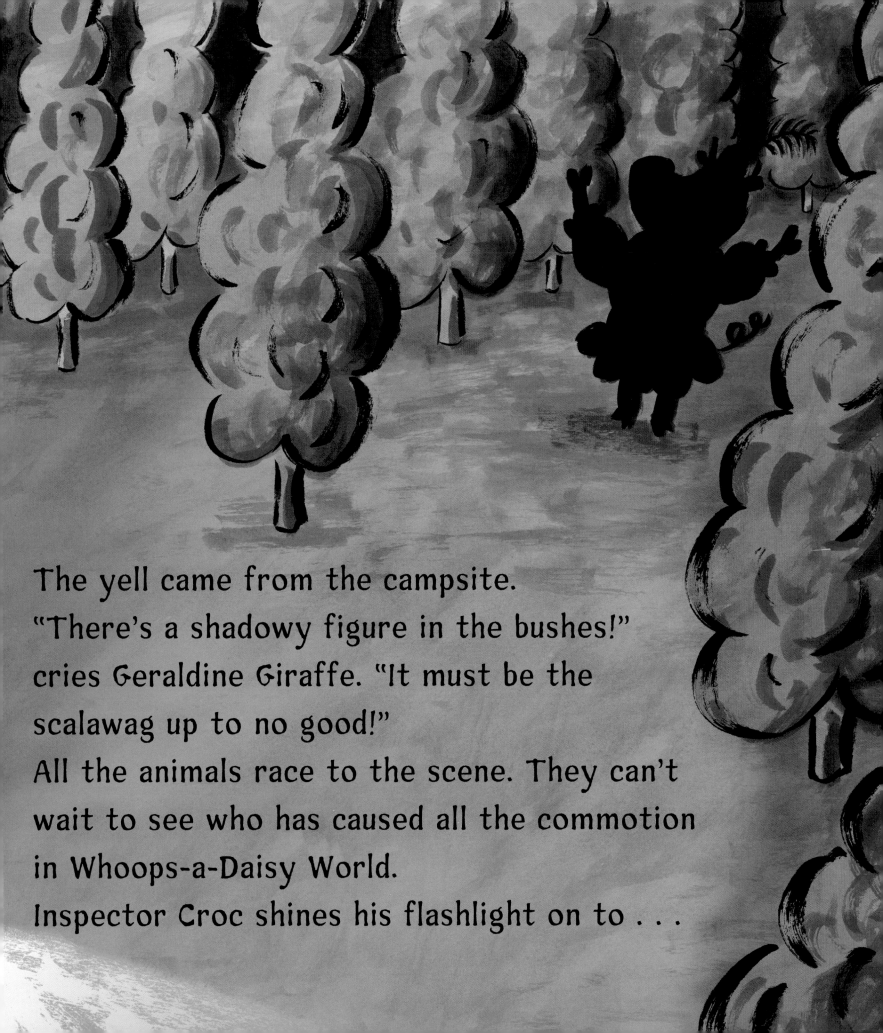

The yell came from the campsite.
"There's a shadowy figure in the bushes!"
cries Geraldine Giraffe. "It must be the
scalawag up to no good!"
All the animals race to the scene. They can't
wait to see who has caused all the commotion
in Whoops-a-Daisy World.
Inspector Croc shines his flashlight on to . . .

. . . Mrs. Piggly!

"Stay calm, ma'am," soothes Inspector Croc.
"You're safe now. Here are your glasses."
"Thank you," sighs Mrs. Piggly. "Without my
glasses I really can't see a thing!"

Inspector Croc explains everything. "All the goings-on today were not the work of a crook but simply Mrs. Piggly's mishaps! She couldn't see the chaos she was causing without her glasses! Sometimes things may seem bad when really they're not."

"So sorry, everyone!" gulps Mrs. Piggly.

At Chill-Out Camp, the animals enjoy
a steaming mug of cocoa.
"To think we thought Mrs. Piggly was
a baddie," they giggle. "Imagine!"

Learn how
to put out
campfires in
this best seller

Fire
safety
Manual

S. Lloyd

Restroom

Now everyone can sleep soundly. Whoops-a-Daisy World is safe once again, thanks to Inspector Croc.